I, Maugin, was once a stone pilot. I have flown through the heart of ice-storms, battled albino rotsuckers over the Mire, fought against sky galleons amidst blazing ironwood pines, the air black with choking smoke . . .

So begins this action-packed tale set in the world of *The Edge Chronicles*.

'Surely in years to come new fantasy creations will be compared with Tolkien, Pratchett and Stewart/Riddell' *School Librarian*

'Entertaining fantasy at its finest . . . exceptionally good value' *TES*

SPECIALLY PUBLISHED FOR
WORLD BOOK DAY 2006

www.kidsatrandomhouse.co.uk/edgechronicles

Praise from readers of *The Edge Chronicles*:

'Your books are the best in the whole universe.'
Huw, Warwickshire

'I was never a big reader until I was given *Beyond the Deepwoods* – for Christmas in 2003. When I started to read it I never stopped or let the book out of my sight! I read the Twig trilogy in seven days!!!'   *Michael, Liverpool*

'I am writing to say how much I love your series *The Edge Chronicles*. The illustrations in your books are really good. I spend as long looking at the details in your pictures as I do reading the book!'   *Zoe, Bury*

'I adore the *Edge Chronicles* books. The illustrations are amazing!'   *Pippa, Herefordshire*

'I was amazed at the constant twists which made me want to read your books. Your writing also inspired me to write better, as a result, I got good marks in English exams. Your books were so exciting and thrilling, I forced my mum to buy all your books. I think my mum was surprised at the speed I read these books! All your books are full of heart-stopping adventure.'   *Karl, London*

'I'm writing to say how much I enjoy your books. They're really exciting and give me many ideas for my own stories. I really enjoy being a member of the *Edge Chronicles* fan club. You are definitely my favourite authors so THANKS for writing!'   *Peter, Glasgow*

'Your books are adventurous, they're exciting and they're packed full with amazingly different creatures; down from a tiny Wig-Wig right to the great Banderbear. Once I start to read one of your books I just can't put it down.'   *Rory, Suffolk*

'Please, please, PLEASE write more as many parts of my brain depend on it!'   *Sophie, Essex*

THE DEEP WOODS

THE TWILIGHT WOODS

THE EDGELANDS

The Edge.

For Jack, Katy, Anna, Joseph and William

THE STONE PILOT
A CORGI BOOK : 978 0 552 554398 (from January 2007)
0 552 55439 1

First publication in Great Britain

Corgi edition published 2006, specially for World Book Day 2006

1 3 5 7 9 10 8 6 4 2

Text and Illustrations copyright © Paul Stewart
and Chris Riddell, 2006

The rights of Paul Stewart and Chris Riddell to be identified as the
authors of this work have been asserted in accordance with the
Copyright, Designs and Patents Act 1988.

Papers used by Random House Children's Books are natural,
recyclable products made from wood grown in sustainable forests.
The manufacturing processes conform to the environmental
regulations of the country of origin.

Set in 10½/15pt Palatino by Falcon Oast Graphic Art Ltd

Corgi Books are published by Random House Children's Books,
61–63 Uxbridge Road, London W5 5SA,
a division of The Random House Group Ltd,
in Australia by Random House Australia (Pty) Ltd,
20 Alfred Street, Milsons Point, Sydney, NSW 2061, Australia,
in New Zealand by Random House New Zealand Ltd,
18 Poland Road, Glenfield, Auckland 10, New Zealand,
and in South Africa by Random House (Pty) Ltd,
Isle of Houghton, Corner Boundary Road
Carse O'Gowrie, Houghton 2198, South Africa

THE RANDOM HOUSE GROUP Limited Reg. No. 954009
www.kidsatrandomhouse.co.uk

A CIP catalogue record for this book is available from the British Library.

Printed and bound in Great Britain by Cox & Wyman Ltd.

THE EDGE CHRONICLES

THE STONE PILOT

PAUL STEWART & CHRIS RIDDELL

CORGI BOOKS

Special publication for World Book Day 2006

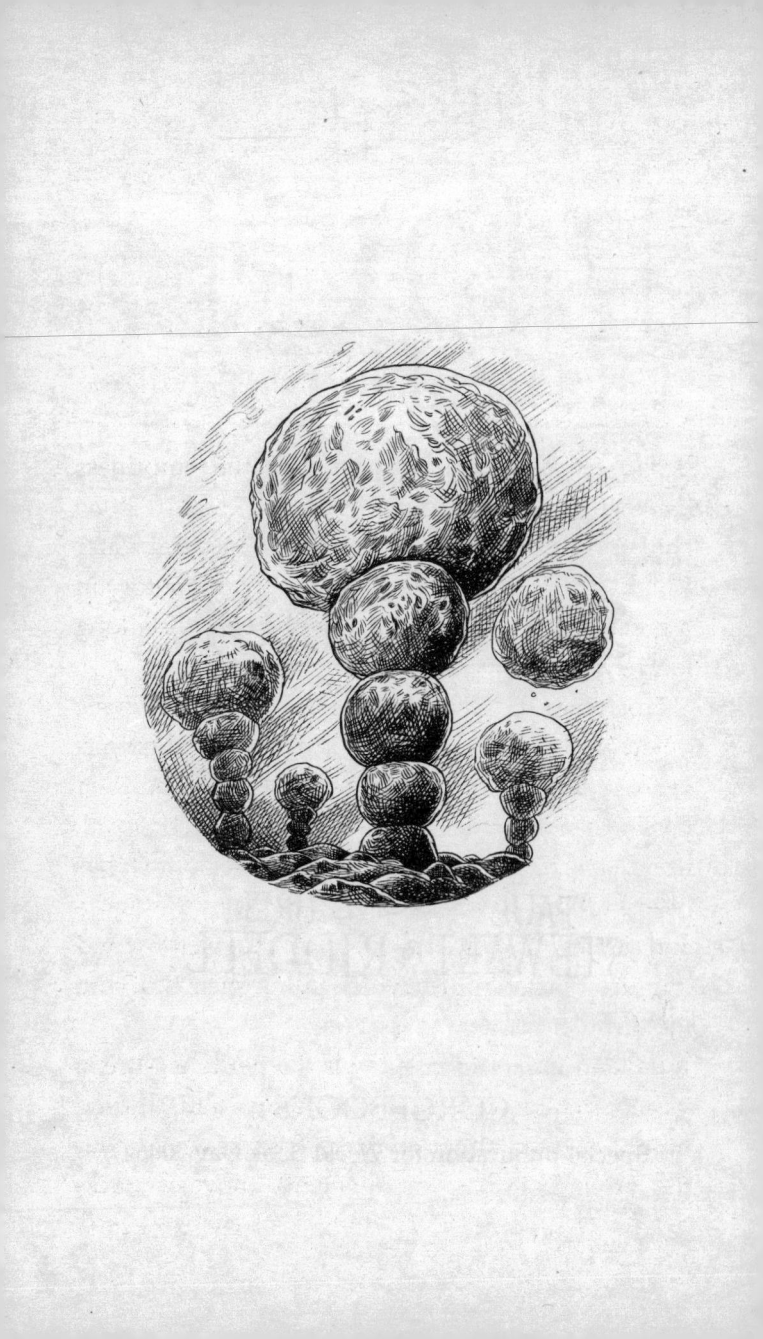

INTRODUCTION

Far, far away, jutting out into the emptiness beyond, like the figurehead of a mighty stone ship, is the Edge. A torrent of water – the Edgewater River – pours down from that lonely promontory in a great, noisy surge that marks the end of its long journey.

Upstream lie the mysterious Stone Gardens, where the buoyant rocks that keep the sky ships airborne grow in tall stacks. On further, and the river passes beneath the greatest buoyant rock of all, upon which the floating city of Sanctaphrax has been built, as it winds its way between the docks and jetties of Undertown, and the factory and foundry outflow pipes which pump their filth into the turbulent water.

Beyond Undertown sprawls the perilous Mire, a vast bleached wasteland of swamps and shifting mudhills. Here, although the river sinks deep under the ground, it has left the land above it pockmarked with areas of sinking-mud and, when the pressure beneath the surface becomes too much, violent blow-holes that erupt with no warning. It is underground, too, when it crosses the Twilight Woods. Some claim that this is because the treacherous half-lit forest – a terrible place which robs those who get lost inside it of their senses and reason, yet denies them the peacefulness of death – allows nothing that enters it to find a way out.

It is only when it reaches the Deepwoods that the river reappears, dividing and sub-dividing into countless tributaries which fan out across the endless forest, gradually making their way back to the source of all the water of the Edge: a place known as Riverrise. It is this maze of waterways – brooks, streams, rivulets, now tumbling down rapids and gushing waterfalls, now sprawling out as wood-midge-infested marshes, now forming deep, crystal-clear lakes – which is the lifeblood of the Edgelands, a lifeblood that attracts creatures in all their various forms.

Waifs and woodtrolls, mobgnomes and clod-dertrogs, and goblins of every type – tusked, tufted, pink-eyed, lop-eared and grey. Some are ferocious, like the warrior hordes of battle-scarred flat-heads and hammerheads. Some are peaceable, like web-footed goblins and their gentle cousins, the gyle goblins. But all of them – each and every one – are dependent on the water that passes through their dark forest homeland.

An explorer to the Deepwoods would discover countless strange creatures – from solitary banderbears to swarms of snickets; from halitoads that kill their prey with noxious breath to logworms that rise up and swallow it whole; from garrulous gabtrolls with their eyes on stalks to bearded prowlgrins; bodies like barrels, legs like a treefrog's and nostrils on the tops of their great round heads.

And perhaps strangest of all, a tribe of creatures that few but the most intrepid explorer could ever hope to encounter. These are among the shyest, most secretive of all the denizens of the Deepwoods – so reclusive and hidden that many scholars doubt their actual existence and believe that they are the stuff of myth and legend.

Such scholars, however, are wrong. This hidden tribe does indeed exist. They are called termagant trogs and, like so many others in the Deepwoods, their history has been passed down from generation to generation by word of mouth. Tales of individual bravery, fortitude, adventure and exploration.

What follows is but one of these tales.

. CHAPTER ONE .

THE PROWLGRIN PUP

I Maugin, was once a stone pilot. I have flown through the heart of ice-storms, battled albino rotsuckers over the Mire, fought against sky galleons amidst blazing ironwood pines, the air black with choking smoke . . . And throughout it all, I kept my sky ship afloat. I must use my skills now, on this sadness that threatens to destroy me. Tend it carefully, bring it back under control and use my memories like the pulleys and levers on a flight-rock platform, just like the stone pilot I once was . . .

I close my eyes, breathe deeply and go back, back to the very beginning, where it all started in the Great Trog Cavern far beneath the Deepwoods. It was there that I, Maugin, daughter of Loess, granddaughter of Loam, great-great-great-granddaughter of Argil, the first Cavern Mother, was born. Today, I am eighty-eight seasons of the bloodoak old, which is, even for termagant trogs, a great age – and yet I look barely twelve.

And that is my great sadness; a sadness I keep wrapped up inside me like a carefully tended flight-rock in a sky-ship cage – sometimes sinking, sometimes rising, but with me always.

Now, as I stand here by the lake of lonely Riverrise and stare out across the endless Deepwoods, my heart grows heavy, like a hot rock heated by the burning flames of memory. And, like a sinking flight-rock, the sadness – that terrible weight at the very centre of my being – is threatening to drag me over the edge and into the black void below, from which there can be no escape . . .

But I must go back to my earliest memories, memories of the wondrous cavern, place of my birth. Tears come to my eyes when I think of it . . .

It was beautiful, so beautiful. Stout, pillar-like roots from the trees growing in the forest up-top spanned the air, from the vaulted ceilings above, down to the soft earth of the cavern floor below – roots that provided for our every need.

As well as the roots of the sacred bloodoak, there were many, many others. Some, like the sweet-lullabee and the yellow-sapwood, provided nourishment; some – ironwood, leadwood and copperwood pines – yielded the raw materials for our dwellings; while others, such as the beautiful wintertree and delicate dew-willow, glowed softly, bathing the cavern in a soothing pastel light.

And then there was the underground lake of crystal-clear dew-water. Beside it, where the tangle of roots fanned out, we trogs built our cabins of paper, piled one upon another to form a trogcomb of dwellings. They were round and snug, separated one from the other by communal walkways, and whenever anyone was home – day or night – each one was lit up from within by flickering root candles.

Oh, how I loved to stand by the dew lake. I would gaze at the shimmering lights of the trogcomb reflected in its still waters, waiting for my beloved mother, Loess, to return from the root harvest.

I can recall her so clearly, even after all these seasons, standing tall in her paper robes, magnificent tattoos covering her strong arms and gleaming bald head. Thin, weedy trog males would trot along beside her, carrying her huge scythe and root-tap, while she carried a trug laden with lullabee shoots and sapwood nectar for our supper. When I saw her, I would let out a cry of delight and rush back to our cabin to light the root candle and spread the paper supper-cloth before she arrived home.

Then, after our meal in that small, glowing dwelling-place, my mother – her papery clothes rustling – would sit me on the floor and comb and plait and bead and braid my hair, all the while telling me stories. Wonderful tales, they were, of the termagant trog sisterhood, and of Argil, the first Cavern Mother, and how she had founded our colony beneath the roots of a sacred bloodoak tree, digging out the first small cavern with her daughters, and creating a tiny dew pond. Safe from the terrors and dangers of the world up-top, the colony prospered, and the cavern grew into the mighty trog cavern I knew so well.

Down there, amidst the glowing roots and glistening lake, there was no snow, no rain, no hurricanes or storms. The cavern sheltered us. It kept us cool when the woods up-top shimmered in the heat, and kept us warm when the ironwood pines groaned beneath layers of snow and ice. And not only did the cavern shelter us, but it protected us as well.

Up-top, as every trog knew, the countless Deepwoods tribes were forever fighting, with pitched battles constantly breaking out as marauding hordes pillaged and ransacked each other's settlements and villages. Fearsome shryke battle-flocks, savage hammerhead goblin war parties and roving bands of slavers preyed on the weak and unwary. And as if that wasn't enough, the terrifying creatures of the forest – from halitoads and hover-worms to wig-wigs and snickets – lay in wait behind every tree and in every shadowy glade.

Hidden away down in our cavern, we trogs remained safe while tribes fought and creatures devoured each other in the world up-top. And if any unwanted visitor got too close to our cavern entrance, then the sacred blookoak – together with its deadly sidekick, the tarry vine – soon took care of them. Most of those up there knew from bitter experience to avoid any glade where a bloodoak had taken root, and we termagant trogs were left in peace to enjoy life in our beautiful caverns far below the hustle and bustle of the world above us.

And so it was that we became the most secretive of all the tribes in the vast Deepwoods. Few up-top had ever seen a termagant trog for themselves. In fact, as I was to discover, there were many who believed that we didn't actually exist at all, but were simply the stuff of old gabtroll tales.

All this I learned as a young trog at my mother's knee, as she combed and braided my beautiful flowing orange hair – hair that we both knew I would lose when I reached my twelfth season of the bloodoak and turned termagant at the Blooding Ceremony. Ah, the Blooding Ceremony! That extraordinary transforming event, which can happen only once in a trog's lifetime . . .

There it is again; the sadness, heavy in my heart – unbearably heavy. I must be careful or it'll sink me. I must try to lighten it; to cool the sadness, like an over-heated flight-rock cooled by the cold earth released bit by bit with the drenching-lever . . .

I know, I'll think of Blink . . .

Yes, that's it. Blink. My darling little prowlgrin pup. He could only have been a few hours old when I first laid eyes on him, nestling in my mother's huge, outstretched hands.

'*There* you are, Maugin, my little dew-blossom,' she said brightly, her bloodshot eyes twinkling as she handed me the little creature. 'I've brought you something.'

I smiled. Although huge and fearsome, termagant trog mothers are exceptionally tender and nurturing to their young. By encouraging their daughters to keep pets they believe that they, in their turn, will become good mothers. Loess was no exception.

'What is it?' I asked.

Gazing up at me through large trusting eyes was a furry orange creature with strong back legs and a huge mouth.

'Up-top they're known as prowlgrins,' Loess smiled. 'This one's a pup. A clutch hatched out in a copperwood pine just above the tunnel mouth, and it fell into one of our nets . . . They make good pets – they're affectionate, easily trained, and we don't have to worry, because they're not talkers.'

We trogs never allowed any creature into our cavern that might give away the secret of our existence.

'It's only a pity that it's a male,' she said, and chuckled. 'What are you going to call him?'

I looked down at the tiny creature, and as I did so, his mouth parted, almost like a smile, and his two great big yellow eyes closed momentarily.

'Blink,' I said. 'I'm going to call him Blink.'

From that day on, Blink and I were inseparable. I fed him on fat pink grubs from the gnarled roots of dew-willows, which he'd only eat after I'd squished them and their wriggling had stopped. Then he'd bark excitedly and wag his thin, whiplash tail while I dropped the slimy things into his gaping mouth.

As Blink quickly grew on his diet of root grubs, we explored every part of the cavern. We would paddle in the dew lake, chase each other through the root clusters and play hide-and-seek amongst the paper cabins of the trogcomb. There was only one place Blink would not go near, and that was the great cluster belonging to the blood-oak, which lay at the very centre of the cavern.

When these roots glowed red, he would yelp with

fear and back away, as if sensing that up-top, the sacred bloodoak was gorging on some unfortunate prey. It was just as well, for pets weren't allowed inside the dome of the root cluster where the taproot grew and the Blooding Ceremony took place . . .

But I must try not to think of that.

Blink's favourite place was below the mouth of the entrance tunnel. Whenever we went there, he'd get excited and skittish and begin to leap high on his powerful legs, his tongue lolling out of his wide mouth and a wild look in his yellow eyes as he sniffed at the air coming in from outside. Sometimes, it was all I could do to drag him away from the entrance tunnel on the end of the sumproot rope I had, by then, taken to attaching to his collar. He was getting stronger by the day.

When I told Loess of his behaviour, she smiled and gently ruffled my hair.

'What you have to remember, my little bloodoak-acorn,' she said, 'is that Blink's natural home is up-top, in the highest of the high treetops. He can sense it calling to him . . .'

'But his home is here with me!' I protested. 'He's *my* Blink, and I love him!'

'Your Blooding Ceremony is soon,' Loess said kindly. 'After that, your feelings will change. You'll have no more time for pets, and you'll be ready to raise a daughter of your own.'

'I'll always love Blink!' I cried, hugging the pup fiercely.

'You've raised him well, but if you want to really prove your love, you'll let him go before you turn termagant,' Loess replied.

I can feel the tears returning to my eyes as I remember my beloved mother's words. She was right, of course. I knew it, even back then, as a young trog of twelve seasons. What I didn't know – couldn't have known – was how this act of love was going to change my life for ever.

I remember it as if it were yesterday. Loess and the trog sisters had examined me, noting that my hair had a deep orange lustre, my white skin a pearly bloom, and that my eyes were glistening brighter and bluer than ever before. I was ready to turn termagant, they declared, and hurried away to prepare the tap-root. My Blooding Ceremony would take place the next day. There remained one last thing to do.

With a heavy heart and trembling fingers, I awoke, took hold of Blink's leash and set off for the cavern's entrance tunnel.

I was taking my darling prowlgrin pup up-top to set him free.

I remember the feel of the sumproot rope in my hands as I gripped it tightly and an increasingly skittish Blink dragged me up the tunnel towards the world above. We brushed past the nets that kept creatures out of the cavern, slipped round a sharp corner and up a gentle slope . . .

And there we were, in a small hollow beneath a curved root of a copper-wood pine, looking out across a sunlit glade. All around were mighty trees and lush Deepwoods vegetation – sallowdrops, dellberry bushes and saw-fronds. But what I remember most – more than the sun's dappled light or the swaying of the trees; more than the hum of woodbees or the distant whooping of a far-off fromp – was the shock of feeling the wind on my face.

Down in the protecting

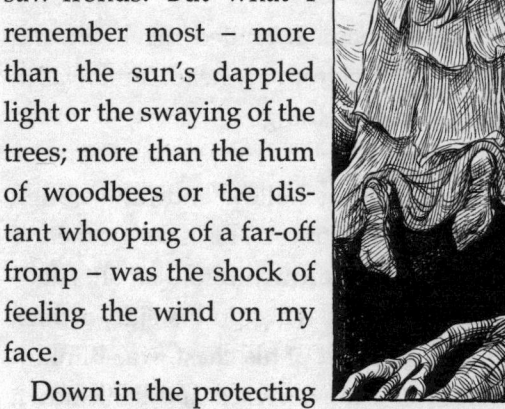

cavern, the air was warm and still. The only breeze was the gentle waft of a paper screen falling across a cabin door. But here, the feeling of wind on my face was shocking, as if I had suddenly shrunk to the size of a seed-head and was about to be blown away into the Deepwoods and lost for ever.

My heart started pounding, I struggled for breath and my knees felt weak. I dropped the sumproot rope – and with a yelp of delight, Blink leaped out into the glade and off through the trees.

'Goodbye, Blink!' I called after him, my head spinning as the pup disappeared from view. 'Goodbye, boy!'

I turned, and was about to stumble back down the tunnel, still shocked by the feel of the wind ruffling my hair and rustling the paper cloak I was wearing, when a sound rang out.

'*Yeeaaoowaargh!*'

It was a howl of pain. It chilled my heart and drove all other thoughts from my head. Blink was in trouble! I had to do something.

I had to help him.

I flung myself from the hollow and ran through the glade and into the trees. The next moment I burst through the undergrowth into a small, shadowy clearing. And there, lying on his side, a thick barbed arrow sticking out of his chest, was Blink.

'No!' I cried out. I ran forward and sank down

beside him, cupping his head in my hands.

The wounded pup looked up at me, his great yellow eyes seeming to appeal to me for help. Then he blinked – once, twice . . . The eyes misted over and the third time they closed, they remained shut.

'Oh, Blink!' I sobbed, scalding tears welling up in my eyes and streaming down my cheeks. 'Blink. Bl—'

Crack!

From behind me came the sound of a breaking twig, followed by a low, rumbling growl. . .

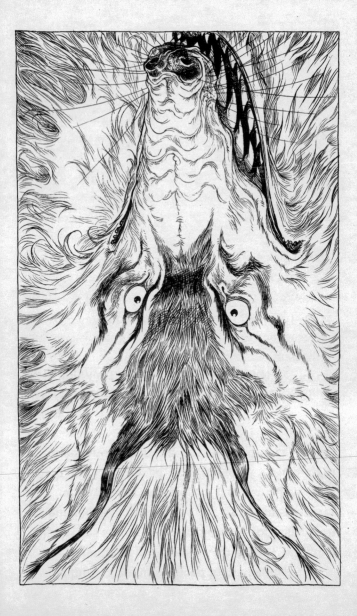

. CHAPTER TWO .

WOODWOLVES

I turned round slowly, hardly daring to breathe, to find myself staring into two glowing yellow eyes. A huge grey creature with tufted ears and glistening fangs was standing at the far edge of the clearing. The great white mane of fur round its throat stood on end as it tensed its powerful legs in readiness to pounce. Unable to tear my eyes from the cruel stare of the great whitecollar woodwolf, I backed slowly away on trembling knees.

From the forest behind the snarling beast came the bloodcurdling howls of the rest of the pack as they picked up the scent of blood. Suddenly, the woodwolf sprang – followed by two, three, four others that burst into the gloomy clearing in a cloud of dust and a swirl of leaves. I let out a high-pitched scream and curled up in a tight ball, expecting at any moment to feel the pain of those terrible fangs tearing into me.

Instead, the clearing filled with the hideous

sounds of snarling and snapping as the savage wolves fell upon the body of Blink, my darling pet. I couldn't bear to look, and instead scrambled to my feet and ran full-pelt from that terrible place, back into the undergrowth.

I kept on running – running till my head pounded, my lungs burned and I feared my heart would burst. I jumped over streams, I leaped fallen logs; I dodged thornbushes and boulders. And as I ran, a terrible panic rose in my chest.

I was lost and alone in this vast, terrible place full of long thorns which scraped and tore at my shoulders and back, and strange plants and berries which released pungent, heady odours as my feet trampled them. And worst of all was the terrifying feel of the wind on my face, making me gasp and sob, and struggle for breath.

At last, exhausted, I could bear it no longer. I collapsed on the forest floor and lay there, tattered and torn and half out of my mind. I wanted to hide, to disappear into the ground and escape from the vast terrifying openness of the world up-top. My fingers clawed at the earth. And as they did so, they released a sickly, rancid odour which made me gag . . .

Behind me, coming closer through the trees, I could hear the snarling growls and excited yelps of the woodwolves. They were following my scent. It wouldn't be long now, I thought to myself, scalding tears running down my cheeks, before I too was torn apart, just like Blink.

Crack! Crack! Crack!

Suddenly there were twigs snapping behind me. I glanced round over my shoulder, and there – coming through the dense undergrowth towards me, moving like water sluicing through sand – were four of the woodwolves.

Their red eyes blazed, their blood-stained nostrils snorted, their tongues – dripping with saliva – lolled over their sabre-like teeth. I could hear them, panting and slavering, their paws pounding, their bodies swooshing through the undergrowth and, as they approached, I could *smell* them, too. The stale odour of their fur. The gagging tang of their rotten-meat breath . . .

I buried my face in my hands, my eyes shut tight, and gasped. The earth beneath me smelled worse than the woodwolves.

'Yarrghaaoow!'

The howling screech slashed through the air like a blunt knife, sending jarring shudders down my neck and spine. I looked up, but didn't understand at first what was happening.

The woodwolf seemed to be *flying*!

The next moment, there was a whistling *swoosh*, and out of the corner of my eye I caught a flash of green. Heart racing, I turned to see a long green tendril wrap itself round the belly of a second woodwolf once, twice, three times, and wrench it from the ground. It followed its hapless companion through the air, yelping and whimpering as it disappeared into the shadows of the forest.

I lay there for a moment, watching the space in the air where the two creatures had been hovering a moment earlier. The other two wolves let out piercing squeals, turned on their heels and fled. Slowly, I got to my feet and looked up.

I was in a glade of dark red earth, flecked with jagged white shards of what I took to be rocks, but which on closer inspection turned out to be bones. At the centre of the clearing stood a colossal tree, its roots sinking down into a great mound of skulls, ribcages and leg bones. Its mighty trunk pulsated with glistening lumps and grotesque nodules, and from the top, where its great branches sprouted, the sound of a thousand mandible-like teeth gnashing filled the air.

'M . . . Mother Bloodoak,' I whispered in awe, sinking to my knees before the sacred tree.

What I witnessed next still fills me with horror and revulsion when I recall it. The two woodwolves were clasped in the deadly embrace of the tarry vine, its thick roots anchored deep in the pulsating trunk of its host, the bloodoak. The whiplash tendrils of the vine raised the unfortunate creatures high in the air and dangled them over the great gaping mouth of the flesh-eating tree. For an instant they hung there, wriggling and writhing and letting out bloodcurdling screaming howls. Then, with a spasm, the vines released the wolves into the tree's gaping maw.

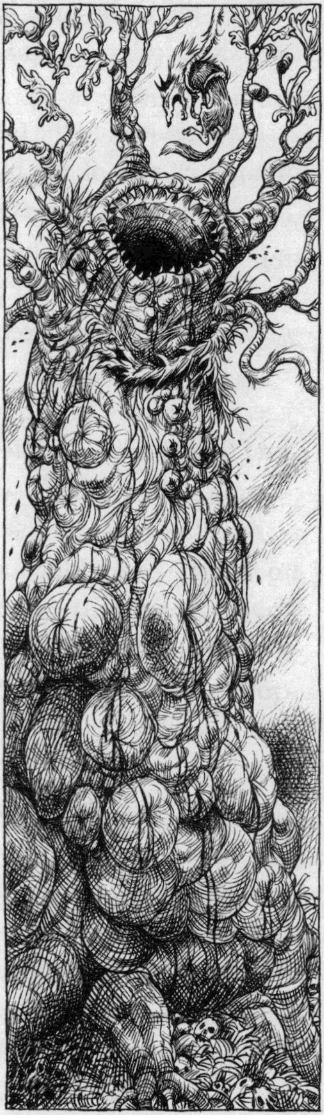

A horrible crunching sound was followed a few moments later by a thick column of blood and bones which exploded from the bloodoak's jaws. The lumps and nodules on the trunk greedily sucked the blood in as it streamed down, the entire tree shuddering and pulsating in sickening convulsions.

Down below, in the Great Cavern, I knew that the domed cluster of the bloodoak would be glowing red as the roots filled with blood, and the sacred tap-root would be bulging. When I was down there, in the beautiful, glowing cavern, I'd never thought of the nightmarish scene unfolding up-top every time the bloodoak fed – the feeding which enabled each Blooding Ceremony to take place. And for the first time, I felt a terrible sadness well up within me – sadness I have lived with now for so long.

As I stood before the sacred bloodoak, I wanted to forget everything, to return to the beautiful cavern of my birth and to my beloved mother, and to wipe all thoughts of the terrible world up-top from my mind. My mother had told me that I'd change when I turned termagant and, standing there in that terrible glade, frightened and alone, that was what I wanted to do more than anything in the world.

I glanced about me, trying to get my bearings. Below my feet, I knew, was the Great Cavern, which meant that the entrance tunnel couldn't be far away. I looked around the glade, searching for the copperwood pine. And there in the distance it stood, its reddish gold branches standing out from the sallowdrop trees all round it.

I raced towards it, running as I'd never run before, panting loudly, my hair streaming out behind me. And as I reached the edge of the glade, I saw a smaller sunlit clearing further on, and the copperwood pine with the shadowy hollow beneath its curving roots.

'The tunnel,' I breathed.

Leaping over a jutting boulder and negotiating the ridges of tree roots poking up through the surface of the earth, I hurried on. Past a lullabee I went, past a bank of jangling flowers. All at once the clearing was before me, drenched in late afternoon sunlight. I rushed into it, happiness welling up inside me. For there,

on the far side, in the hollow beneath the roots of the copperwood pine, was the entrance.

'Mother,' I gasped, stumbling those last few strides. 'I'm coming. . .'

But then, just as I was crossing the clearing, there was a flurry of movement in front of me and two of the woodwolves stepped out from the shadows. They barred my path, their fangs bared and the white hair around their necks standing on end.

I skidded to a halt, terror screaming in every pore of my body. Desperately, I looked around.

Four more woodwolves appeared at the edges of the clearing, one to my left, one to my right and the other two behind me. I was surrounded by the pack. Once again I found myself staring into the cruel yellow eyes as the creatures advanced towards me, the circle growing smaller, like the tightening of a noose.

Then, above the low rumble of the woodwolves' throaty growls, I heard another sound. Higher-pitched. Metallic . . .

Clink! Clink! Clink!

. CHAPTER THREE .

ZELT PINK-EYE

'Well, well, well,' came a rough, brutish voice. 'What have my clever boys caught for me *this* time?'

At the sound of the voice, the woodwolves pricked their ears and whimpered eagerly. I looked up and saw, towering over me, the strangest figure I'd ever seen. He was tall and stooped, with incredibly long, spindly legs and arms, and huge hands with thin spidery fingers. His body was completely round, and he had almost no neck. Beneath the layers of grime, his face was as white as snow, except for one brown blotch that extended from above his left eye to halfway down his cheek. The eye set within this brown patch was milky – like a pebble in a stream. The other was pink.

He was wearing a long jacket made up of hundreds of different patches, each the skin of a Deepwoods creature – some mottled, some spotted, others soft and furry, or striped and feathery – all patched together in a sort of quilt. From the heavy leather belt around his circular belly hung dozens of traps, snares, collars and chains which clinked gently when he moved.

'Easy, boys,' he growled. 'Don't damage the merchandise.'

Five of the six woodwolves took a step back. The sixth, a hungry glint in its eye, took a step towards me, its teeth bared.

'Tozer!' grunted the strange figure angrily, one of his huge hands straying to his belt. 'Easy, I say!'

Suddenly, his hand snapped forward. It was gripping a coiled whip which swished through the air and landed with a loud *crack* on the woodwolf's snout. The creature yelped and fell back with the others, eyeing me resentfully as it did so.

'That's more like it,' he said. His eyes narrowed. 'Now, let's have a look at you.'

Leering unpleasantly, he swaggered forwards and broke through the circle of woodwolves – tickling the one he'd just punished behind the ear as he did so. It nuzzled against him and licked his palm.

'So, little one,' he said, turning his attention to me, 'what in the name of Earth and Sky is a tiny little slip of a thing like you doing out here in the middle of the Deepwoods? Why, there isn't a village or settled glade for miles.'

Reaching out, he took me gently by the arm and helped me to my feet. I shuddered as a gust of wind blew through the glade, rustling my paper cape and ruffling my hair.

'My, my, but you're a delicate little thing,' he crooned, tilting his great mottled head to one side and eyeing me up and down with his one good eye. 'Old Zelt will have to treat you gentle like.' He gave a wheezing laugh and snapped a delicate pair of manacles around my wrists.

I tried to cry out, to beg him to let me go – but I could not. It was as if the wind had blown my voice away, and however hard I tried, up here in the great vastness of the world up-top, I was unable to make a sound.

He looked around, his good eye narrowing suspiciously. 'I can't see no sign of clan or kin, can you, boys?'

The woodwolves yelped and nuzzled round Zelt's spindly legs.

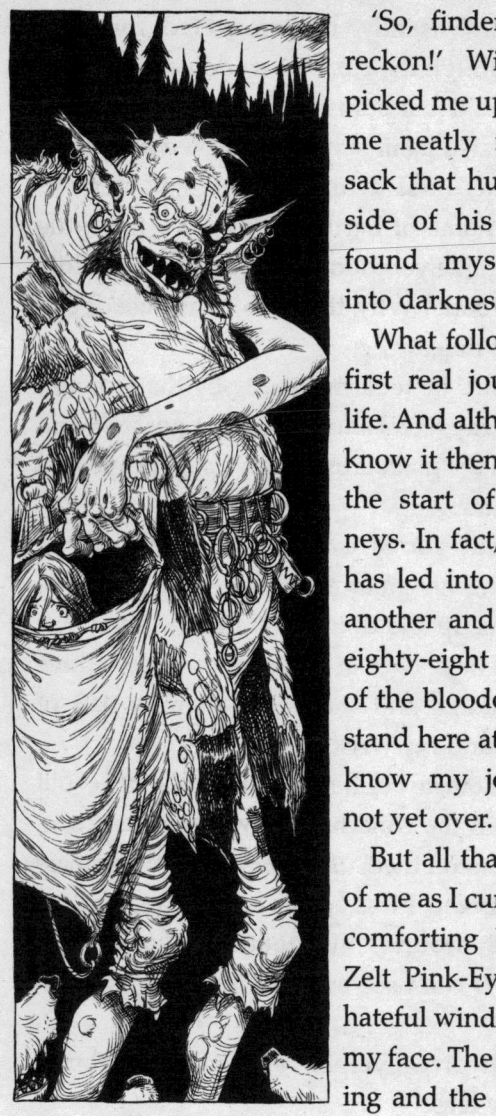

'So, finders keepers, I reckon!' With that, he picked me up and slipped me neatly into a great sack that hung from one side of his belt, and I found myself plunged into darkness.

What followed was the first real journey of my life. And although I didn't know it then, it was to be the start of many journeys. In fact, one journey has led into another and another and even now – eighty-eight long seasons of the bloodoak later, as I stand here at Riverrise – I know my journeying is not yet over.

But all that lay in front of me as I curled up in the comforting blackness of Zelt Pink-Eye's sack, the hateful wind no longer on my face. The steady swaying and the heavy tramp

40

told me I was being carried ever further from my beautiful cavern home.

As he walked, Zelt hummed tunelessly and whistled to his wolves, and the traps and snares on his belt clinked. In the depths of the sack, I felt great waves of sorrow break over me.

I thought of my beloved mother, Loess, in our glowing cabin in the trogcomb, and how she would be preparing my paper robes ready for the Blooding Ceremony. I pictured the sisterhood gathering in the dome of the Bloodoak Root Cluster and making ready the tap-root.

And as I imagined their faces – the pain and worry and distress etched into their features as they searched in vain for me in the cavern – tears welled up in the corners of my eyes and trickled down over my cheeks, and silent sobs racked my body. They would be calling for me to come quickly, their cries ever more desperate, for they knew as well as I that a trog who misses her Blooding Ceremony will never get another chance to turn termagant. I was sobbing freely now, and the trickle of tears had turned to a flood.

Suddenly, I was absurdly grateful to the slaver's sack which, for now at least, shielded me from the terrible world up-top.

'Here, Tozer! Filzer! Ribb!' the slaver's muffled voice sounded, calling to the wolves.

And from outside, I heard the woodwolves whimper and snarl with agitation as the slaver used his whip to bring them to heel.

I don't know how long we travelled. One hour? Three hours? Six . . . ? Locked up inside the darkness of the sack, it was impossible to tell. But although I couldn't see, I could sense the changing ground over which Zelt tramped, by listening to the sound of his great heavy feet – now slapping down on rock, now scrunching over sand, now soft and padded on thick grass growing in soft, loamy-smelling soil. Every footstep he took was transformed into a visual image of our surroundings as the dense forest gave way to glades and clearings, which turned to marshland, pasture, scree, and back again.

Moreover, despite the thickness of the coarse sack, I could sense smells – and even colours. The earthy dampness and the lush greenness of crushed meadow grass; the dusty smell of gravel, acrid, dry and grey; the peaty, rich brown odour of muddy marshland. And as I lay in that swaying sack, I realized that I possessed talents of perception that I hadn't noticed before in my comfortable cavern home.

Despite all this, here in the darkness, it was of course my ears that gave me the most information on the world we travelled through. I could hear a rising wind in the trees, the coming and going of babbling streams, the low moans and muffled sighs of the woodwolves which trotted after us . . . And, above it all, soft yet insistent, the *clink, clink, clink* of the collection of traps and snares hooked to the slaver's belt.

I had no idea of our destination, yet the further we went, the more I dreaded ever reaching it.

It was later – much later – when I heard voices in the distance. I'd grown used to the solitary nature of our march, and the sound made me instantly uneasy. One was shouting; giving orders and barking commands. Others sounded lost and frightened. There were plaintive denials and tearful pleas . . .

As we got closer, I picked up the smell of blazing torches dipped in pine-resin and wax, and braziers stuffed full of oily timber that gave off thick, pungent smoke. The voices grew louder and Zelt's gruff voice rang out in greeting.

'What's all this? Leaving without me, Griddle?'

A thin wheedling voice sounded in reply. 'Of course not, Zelt, me old mate. Just harnessing the hammelhorns to save time. We'll set off at daybreak.'

Zelt gave a throaty laugh, and there was the sound of one of his great hands slapping a back.

'So, what took you so long, Zelt?' Griddle asked. 'Can't be much merchandise out there, so far from

43

the settled glades.'

'You never can tell, Griddle,' came the reply, and I felt the sack lurch as Zelt unhooked it from his clinking belt. 'What do you make of this, eh?'

The sack gave another lurch and I tumbled out onto the soft, dusty earth of a forest clearing. It was dark and, all around, burning torches cast nightmarish shadows over the great wooden wagon and squat, hairy beasts in harness before me. A small goblin with a pointy, twitching nose thrust his face into mine and narrowed his small, cruel-looking eyes.

'Darned if I know, Zelt,' he hissed. 'Still, let's get it loaded. Everything's got to be ready. If we don't leave at daybreak, the merchandise is going to start dying on us before we reach market.'

With that, he grabbed me roughly by the arm and dragged me towards the great gaping door of the wagon.

'Careful, Griddle!' Zelt protested, hurrying behind. 'Don't damage it. It's a delicate little thing . . .'

'*Pah!*' snapped Griddle, flinging me roughly through the door, into the fetid, inky blackness. 'Perhaps *too* delicate, Zelt, me old mate,' he hissed, slamming the heavy wooden door shut, 'for the bidding hook!'

. CHAPTER FOUR .

THE SLAVE WAGON

That night and the following day were among the strangest of my long life. It was there, in the darkness of that foul-smelling slave wagon, that I learned much of the evils of the world up-top, and shed bitter tears for the cavern life I now knew I was leaving behind for ever. For even if I was to escape and find my way back to the cavern, I had now missed my Blooding Ceremony and would never turn termagant. I was an outcast.

The wagon was full of the 'merchandise' I'd heard Zelt Pink-Eye and his partner, Griddle, talk of. They settled themselves outside, at the front of the covered wagon, on comfortable seats from which they whipped the hammelhorns into motion as the first light of dawn broke. From the dark, stuffy interior, we could hear them laughing and joking and passing a bottle of woodgrog back and forth between them as they boasted of what fine specimens they'd secured for the bidding hook.

At each mention of that dreaded contraption, I felt my heart flutter, and even now – all these seasons later – the sound of those two little words still fills me with dread. And I clearly wasn't the only one. As my eyes became accustomed to the gloom, I began to make out the features of the merchandise around me, and catch snatches of their whispered conversation.

It seemed that every Deepwoods tribe and creature was represented in that wagon – and many I have since become familiar with. But back then, when I was a mere slip of a trog of twelve seasons, they were all so strange and wonderfully exotic. There were ghostwaifs, even smaller than me, with huge fluttering ears and big sad eyes. Crimson-haired slaughterers huddled next to tousle-haired woodtrolls; gnokgoblins and tree goblins cowered beside sad, weeping mobgnomes . . .

'I was out fishing when it happened,' someone close by was saying. 'Terrible bad luck.' The voice sounded friendly, I thought, soft and with a lilting burr. 'Course I'm not blaming her, but if my Rilpa hadn't said how much she fancied a little bit of sweetwater chubbock for her supper, I wouldn't have been there, rod, hook, net and a pot full of woodbottle grubs in hand.'

The axles squeaked and the timbers creaked as the lumbering wagon continued across the bumpy forest floor, jolting and jarring us as the ironwood wheels seemed to find every tree-root and boulder in the pitted track.

'Went down to a place we mobgnomes know as Mogred's Elbow, I did,' the voice went on. 'A great deep pool at a bend in the Edgewater River. Sat me down 'neath a spreading sallowdrop tree. It was warm, peaceful, my eyelids grew heavy ... Next thing I know, I've been caught, and in me own net. Me *own net*! Can you believe it?'

Whoever it was that he was telling his story to must have muttered something sympathetic in response, but I didn't catch what it was.

'That weaselly little goblin caught me. All bones and sinews – and he had a vicious whip,' he added, and I could hear the pain in his voice. 'Clapped me in irons and dragged me away.' He paused for a moment. 'What on Earth are Rilpa and the young'uns gonna do without me?'

To my left, other voices – three of them – were arguing.

'This is what comes from seeking new pastures.' The voice sounded tetchy.

'But the tilder-grazing there was perfect – sweet young meadowgrass.'

'It might have been sweet, but it was too far from the village hammocks. I warned you, Glottis, but you wouldn't listen. You never do . . .'

'Come on, now,' broke in a third voice, older and wearier than the others. 'He didn't do it on purpose.'

'I never said he did. All I know is that if we hadn't taken the herd so far away, this would never have happened.'

'Well, it's no good crying over spilt tildermilk, Spleen,' said the older slaughterer. I could just see his sad, red face in the gloom as he turned to his companions. 'And at least we led the slavers away from the village . . .'

As the wagon rumbled on, I found myself listening to someone else – a young woodtroll who was seated some way to my right. He looked about my age, and was being comforted by the strangest individual in the whole wagon – a creature with large flapping ears and eyes on the ends of stalks, which she kept moist with her long, slurping tongue as she talked. It was my first sight of a gabtroll, and I'll never forget her.

'In your own . . . *slurp* . . . time, m'dear,' she whispered. 'And don't fret yourself.'

'It's like I said,' the frightened woodtroll's voice whispered back. 'I did what I shouldn't do – what *no* woodtroll should do, let alone a young'un. I strayed from the path.'

The gabtroll patted his shoulder gently.

'We were out mushroom-gathering. Me, my big sister Briary and cousin Towselbark, each of us with a plaited trug that we were racing to fill first. Course, we were sticking to the path, only venturing off a few steps after mushrooms if we could actually *see* a clump growing.'

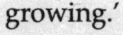

'I understand . . . *slurp* . . .'

'Anyway, Briary and I started arguing. She reckoned half of the stuff I'd picked was inedible. Toadstools, she said they were. Poisonous toadstools. And she started tossing them away. I got so upset, that . . . that . . .'

'There, there, now . . . *slurp* . . . It's all right.'

'But it's *not* all right, is it?' the young'un sobbed. 'I ran off; I strayed from the path . . . That'll show her, I thought. Now she'll be sorry. But the only one I showed was me!' As the hushed whispers continued, I could tell that the woodtroll's tears were flowing freely now, and I felt tears spring into my own eyes. 'I was running across this stretch of ground when – *whumpf!* – this net I'd stepped onto was triggered. It hurtled up into the air with me inside it. The drawstring pulled shut and I was left, dangling from a branch, high up in the air, wrapped up so tightly inside the net I could barely breathe, let alone cry out for help . . .' He sniffed. 'Two days I hung there. No one found me – until the slaver came. Cut me down, he did. Tossed me into a sack and slung me from his belt . . .'

Suddenly, it all became too much for me and I burst into tears. The gabtroll shuffled over and ran a stubby hand over my head.

'Oh, my dear,' she soothed. 'Don't take on so . . .

My, but you're a delicate little one ... *slurp!* Well I never!' Her stalk-like eyes came towards me and looked me up and down. 'Why, as I live and breathe, you're ... *slurp* ... a termagant trog!'

I nodded tearfully.

The gabtroll gave me a comforting hug. It was almost as if I were back with my beloved mother Loess, and I could barely control my sobs.

'There, there,' soothed the gabtroll. '*Slurp* ... Well, you're a rare one and that's a fact ... And not turned termagant, I see ... *Slurp* ...'

I looked up, startled that she should know so much. She seemed almost to be able to read my thoughts.

'Oh, my poor, poor dear!' She shook her head.

'By the look of you, you were ... *slurp* ... almost due for your blooding.'

I nodded.

'Standing beneath the tap-root of the mighty bloodoak, bathing in and drinking deep of its transforming blood ... We gabtrolls are famous for our remedies and potions, but nothing we possess can match the power of the ... *slurp* ... Blooding Ceremony.'

Her strange, stalk-like eyes took on a faraway look for a moment.

'What incredible power ... *slurp* ... to transform a delicate wee creature like yourself into ... *slurp* ... a magnificent trog sister before your very eyes. Your tiny arms swelling with muscles, your legs becoming huge, your beautiful orange hair falling from your head. What an amazing sight that would be ...'

She squeezed me tight.

'And now, my little one, you will never turn termagant ... *slurp*. Oh, my dear ... *slurp* ... I'm so, so sorry. But you must promise me one thing!'

Her whispered voice became suddenly fierce and her eyes blazed.

'Never, ever reveal what you are to anyone else. *Slurp!* Or you'll put yourself in terrible danger, for there are those who would stop at nothing to get their hands on a creature such as yourself – a fabled

54

trogdaughter of the bloodoak. Especially . . .
slurp . . .'

I'll never forget how her eyes bored into mine.
'Especially where *we're* going!'

Just then, the wagon gave a sickening lurch and
came to a shuddering halt.

. CHAPTER FIVE .

THE BIDDING HOOK

The door of the slave wagon crashed open and a blinding shaft of daylight cut through the stale air. Gasps and moans around me mingled with smells and sounds coming from outside. Sizzling meat, sweat, leather, pine-resin smoke, clinking metal, mewing cries of tilder and hearty bellows of hammelhorn were all mixed together in a terrifying concoction that left me trembling with fear.

One by one, the merchandise was hauled out of the wagon by Zelt or Griddle to be greeted by excited shouts or derisory boos from the unseen crowd outside. Nothing I'd seen or heard in the terrible world up-top could have prepared me for this moment.

As the gabtroll – that dear, sweet-hearted creature – was dragged out by her manacled hands, she managed to whisper a few last words to me.

'Courage, little one!' she slurped. 'And remember! Tell no one . . . *slurp* . . . your secret!'

57

She disappeared out through the wagon doorway and a great roar went up, followed by a chorus of excited shouts. A short while later, Zelt Pink-Eye's face loomed over me, a leering smile plastered across it.

'Always sell well, gabtrolls do!' He smirked and grabbed my arm with his huge hands. 'Your turn now, little missy. The bidding hook awaits!'

I screwed my eyes tight shut as he dragged my trembling body out into the light and, as his grip tightened, I felt myself being raised high in the air. There was a ripping sound as my paper cloak snagged on something, and suddenly I felt myself hanging in the air. It is a sensation I will never forget – I felt sickened, vulnerable and utterly helpless . . .

Then I opened my eyes – and immediately wished I hadn't. The sight that greeted me was the most terrifying yet. I was suspended from a great jagged hook that jutted out from a gnarled iron-wood post, high above a great sea of faces gazing up at me.

There were massive ring-collared goblins with tattooed faces, battle-scarred cloddertrogs with heavy brows and twisted smiles, flinty-eyed merchants in high chimney-stack hats and sky pirates wearing heavy coats bedecked with glinting brass instruments. For a moment, there was a hush, before a puzzled hum grew as the crowd began muttering to each other.

Below me, a tall figure in a tattered fromp-fur coat and wide, low-brimmed hat leaned forward from a raised platform and bellowed at the upturned faces.

'And now we come to the last item. From the slave wagon of Zelt Pink-Eye and Griddle Rittblatt...'

He turned and scrutinized me. I can still remember his fat, mottled face – the stubby, upturned nose, the moist red lips and pudgy cheeks with their oiled and plaited side whiskers ... I shudder now as I did then when I recall it.

'A fine, delicate specimen of a ... a...' He seemed lost for words. 'Well, let's just say a forest-dweller. Now who'll start

the bidding at fifty? Fifty, anyone?' He scanned the faces in the crowd.

I looked down at the upturned faces gawping up at me – my own face flushed with a mixture of shame and growing terror.

'Funny little thing, ain't she,' someone near the front commented, elbowing the short, stocky goblin by his side and sniggering.

'Wouldn't last five minutes on furnace duty by the look of her,' opined someone else, who was dressed in thick, stiff clothing.

'No, and not much use at chopping logs, neither,' said his neighbour with a rueful shake of his head.

'Forty?' suggested the auctioneer. 'Thirty . . . ? Twenty? Come on, someone's got to offer me twenty.'

'I wouldn't have the first idea what to do with her,' a merchant in a tall, conical hat muttered with a sneer.

I hung my head as I swayed gently to and fro from that awful hook and wished that I'd been torn to pieces by the woodwolves just like my beloved prowlgrin pup, Blink. Anything was better than this. Just then, a thin hissing voice rang out that made my blood run cold.

'Eight.'

I searched the crowd. A tall, gaunt figure in a tri-corn hat with glowing sumpwood burners attached

to it was staring at me
through small gold-rimmed
spectacles. His eyes were of
the clearest, iciest blue, and
seemed to bore into me, chill-
ing me to the core.

'Eight?' the auctioneer
replied.

The figure nodded, sending
two thin puffs of sumpwood
smoke spiralling into the air.

'Eight, I'm bid,' the auctioneer announced. 'Any
advance on eight?'

The lumpen faces stared back blankly. I willed
someone – *anyone* – to bid against the terrible cold-
eyed character whose stare never wavered for an
instant from my face. But no one did so.

'Eight, going once . . . Going twice . . . Sold to . . .
to . . .'

'Ilmus Pentephraxis,' he announced, striding
through the crowd towards the front. He tossed a
small purse at the auctioneer, and Zelt Pink-Eye
took me down from the bidding hook and handed
me over with a rueful smile.

'Such a delicate little thing,' he muttered, shaking
that mottled head of his. 'Thought you'd go for
more than that. You live an' learn, an' that's a fact.

So long, little one.' He turned away, and as he did so, I heard his parting words. 'Rather you than me.'

The figure in the tricorn hat ignored him, and dug his bony fingers into my arm as he marched me roughly through the crowd, muttering in his thin, reedy voice as he did so.

'Quite a bargain . . . Quite a bargain,' he repeated over and over to himself.

We made our way across the slippery mud towards the edge of the ragged, forlorn forest clearing. And it was from there, in the distance, that I saw an amazing sight. Tethered to the tops of ironwood pines from great circular anchor rings, were great floating sky ships – the first I had ever seen. The sight took my breath away and I must have stopped in my tracks open-mouthed, for I suddenly felt my new owner's fingers digging viciously into my arm and his voice hissing in my ear.

'That's right, my little bargain! Take a good look! We're bound for Undertown, you and I, aboard that fine league ship up there.' He breathed in noisily, greedily, like a hoverworm closing in on its prey. 'You have no idea how long I have searched for a specimen like you. . .'

An evil leer spread across his face and he reached up with his bony fingers and took one of the sump-wood burners from his hat.

'A termagant trog that has yet to turn . . .' The

way he said those words made my knees tremble, and I felt as if I was going to faint. 'You, my little bargain, are unimaginably valuable, did those fools back there in the market but realize.' He chuckled. 'The secrets that you can reveal under the right – how shall I put it? – *experimentation*, could be of incalculable worth. I have a workshop waiting, bloodoak acorns, furnaces, blood . . .'

He traced a finger across the line of my chin and I could feel the sumpwood burner's heat on my cheek, bringing tears to my eyes.

'I shall unlock the secrets of termagantation, my little bargain, and you shall help me . . . The torments shall be exquisite!'

The sumpwood burner

63

touched my skin and I let out a high-pitched scream of pain.

'Hey! *Hey!* You there!' a voice rang out. 'What do you think you're doing?'

Both of us turned to see a young sky pirate, his face flushed and his dark eyes flashing angrily, come striding towards us.

'Mind your own business, you impudent young whelp,' spat Ilmus Pentephraxis, dropping the sumpwood burner and rounding on the sky pirate. 'She is my property, and I'll treat her as I see fit—*Ooomph!*' he gasped as the sky pirate's fist crunched into his midriff.

The leaguesman folded over double, only for the sky pirate to bring a knee up and connect with his jaw. Ilmus crashed down, face first into the mud, and the remaining sumpwood burner fizzled and bubbled as it sank into the ooze.

'Come, little one,' the sky pirate said, flinging a handful of gold coins at the leaguesman. 'I've just purchased your freedom. You can't stay here – it's far too dangerous. You'd better come with me.'

I squinted up into the light through my parted hair to see a tall, handsome youth looking back down at me, his right hand outstretched. His hair was dark and wavy, his skin sallow, his eyes deepest indigo.

And he was smiling. It was the first smile I'd seen since I'd left the Great Trog Cavern. I smiled back and took his hand.

'My name's Quint,' he said as he shook my hand. 'Quint Verginix.'

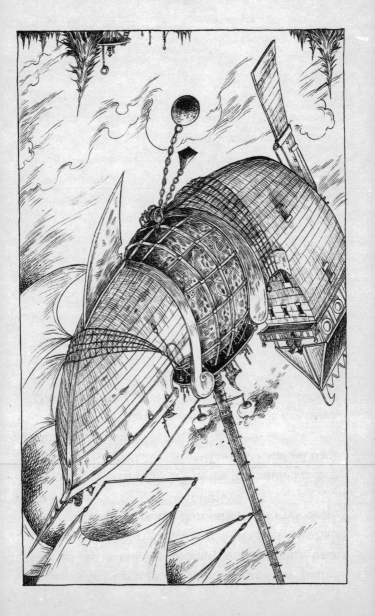

. CHAPTER SIX .

THE SCOURGE OF THE WEAK

Even after all this time, I still find it difficult to describe my emotions as I set foot for the first time on the sky ship that was to become my home. The *Galerider* was a beautiful vessel, a sleek single-master with a fine prow and flying keel. She had a gabled helm at her stern and a wide, circular flight-rock platform in her centre, with meticulously weighted cooling-levers and an ornately decorated rock furnace.

Oh, how I loved that flight-rock platform with its earth buckets and rock-bellows, its cooling rods and heating tongs – tools of what was to become my trade; the trade of the stone pilot.

But, as a dazed, frightened young trog, a mere twelve seasons of the bloodoak old, I noticed none of these things. All I knew was that I was in yet another terrifying place in the world up-top, just as appalling in its own way as the bloodoak glade, the fetid slave wagon or the horrible bidding hook. I was a termagant trog, raised in the security and comfort of the underground cavern, and now I was being helped from a rope-chair onto the foredeck of a sky ship by a young sky pirate.

The wind in my face, ruffling my hair and tugging at my tattered paper cloak, was almost too much to bear. And I remember sinking to my knees and curling up into a terrified ball on the foredeck, just below the flight-rock platform.

A young girl – whom I later came to know as the wise, beautiful Maris, daughter of the late Most High Academe of Sanctaphrax and truest, most devoted friend a termagant trog could ever have – knelt beside me and stroked my trembling head. A moment later, I heard a throaty laugh and looked up to see a tall sky pirate captain smiling down at me. This was my first sight of the great Captain Wind

Jackal. He turned to his son, Quint, a look of indulgent amusement on his face.

'Another one of your waifs and strays, son?' he said. 'I swear you seem to find one in every skyforsaken Deepwoods clearing we put in to.'

Quint smiled back, but there was a serious look in his dark eyes.

'No, Father, not *every* clearing,' he said. 'But I couldn't leave young Tem Barkwater to be flogged back there in the Timber Glades, could I?'

He nodded towards a malnourished youth who was skulking in the shadows of the quarterdeck, just behind Maris. Little did I suspect that that youth was to become one of my closest and most loyal comrades.

'And as for this little one,' Quint continued, turning his attention to me. 'I'd just gone to see about those provisions, and was coming straight back – just like you told me – when I practically tripped over a brute of a leaguesman torturing her. I had to do something!'

'Slave markets are bad places, son. You can't rescue the whole world. Still, what's done is done. We'd better get out of here before you get yourself into any more trouble.' Throwing back his head, he bellowed, 'To your posts!'

All about me, the crew of the *Galerider* ran to their stations and prepared to set sail.

Captain Wind Jackal took the helm, with Quint, his son and my rescuer, by his side. The quartermaster, Filbus Queep, locked the cargo-hold doors with a large brass key which he wore on a chain around his thin neck. Spillins, an ageing oakelf, climbed to his lonely lookout point in the caternest at the top of the mast. Steg Jambles, a bluff, bearded foredecker, and his mate Ratbit, a wiry, swivel-eyed mobg-nome, manned the great harpoon, while the terri-fying Garum Gall – a monstrous cloddertrog with as many tattoos as my mother, Loess – sharp-ened his razor-edge spear on the ironwood gun-wales.

And then there was Ramrock, the stone pilot,

standing above me on the flight-rock platform in his tall, conical hood, heavy gauntlets and apron, firing up the rock furnace and cooling the flight-rock. I shall never forget what happened next, not if I live to be two hundred seasons old.

Captain Wind Jackal gave the command to 'Release the tolley-rope, Steg!' and 'Full lift to the flight-rock, Stone Pilot!' and the mighty sky ship rose up from the mooring rings at the top of the ironwood pines and took to the skies. My stomach lurched and my head spun and tingled. Soon, the ragged, muddy scar in the midst of the Deepwoods that was the evil slave market was far below, and the *Galerider* was soaring off through the clouds.

The terrifying gusts of wind that filled her sails cut right through me and threatened to drive me insane. I was saved from flinging myself to destruction in a fit of sky-madness by one thing – the bright, searing rock furnace burning in its cradle attached to the mast above my head. Its heat seemed to draw me to it, acting as a counter to the horrible feel of the wind on my face.

Almost despite myself, I found I was leaving Maris on the foredeck and climbing up to the flight-rock platform to be closer to its comforting heat. There, I found Ramrock, the stone pilot, urgently going about his profession.

'Sky ship to starboard,' came the high-pitched voice of the oakelf in the caternest. 'A thousand strides and closing.'

Captain Wind Jackal raised the great brass telescope that he kept strapped to his breast-plate and gave a bitter laugh.

'Another one of those bullying league ships by the look of it, with a name to match. Crewed by the dregs of Undertown and captained by a scoundrel, no doubt. Here, take a look.'

He passed the telescope to his son.

'Sky above!' Quint exclaimed. 'He's the one I knocked out in the slave market, Father!'

'Well, whoever our little guest is, he certainly wants her back,' Wind Jackal replied. 'Why, he's brought half the thugs from the market with him!'

'Do we stand and fight, Father?' Quint asked him. 'The Knights Academy trained me well.'

'Only if we have to, son,' laughed his father. 'The *Galerider* will give the *Scourge of the Weak* a run for its league-ship money first!'

'Eight hundred strides, and closing!' Spillins shouted.

'Come on, you scurvy lot,' Wind Jackal bellowed at his crew, his hands darting over the bone-handled flight-levers. 'I need lift and speed. Ramrock, get that rock cooled. Steg, Ratbit – see to the studsail.'

'Six hundred strides,' shouted Spillins.

'By Sky, he's keen,' Wind Jackal said. 'Master Queep, defend the prow. Steg, Ratbit, the foredeck is yours!' He turned to his son. 'Watch my back, Quint, my boy. If it comes to it, they'll attack the helm first!'

'Five hundred strides!'

Maris called up to me to join her below deck, but I couldn't move. I was transfixed. My eyes were on Ramrock with his great hooded coat, his heavy boots and gauntlets, tending to the huge buoyant flight-rock as tenderly as if it were a living, breathing thing – which, as we sped across the sky, I was beginning to see that it was.

As Ramrock pumped the rock-bellows here, and prodded with the cooling rods there, the rock expanded and pressed against the rock cage with a gentle hiss, lifting the sky ship ever higher in the sky. By cooling the flight-rock, the sky ship rose; by heating it, the flight-rock sank, and I soon saw that the flight-rock platform was at the very heart of the little world of the sky ship – and, what's more, that I felt strangely at home there.

'One hundred strides and closing in fast on the port side,' Spillins called down.

I glanced round, and there – horribly close, and getting closer with every passing second – was Ilmus Pentephraxis's league ship, the *Scourge of the Weak*.

It was a heavy-prowed, twin-masted vessel, with double-rigged side sails and a sharp, evil-looking keel. Although the *Galerider* was both sleeker and more elegant, the league ship had twice as much sail and was rapidly catching her.

With the league ship fast approaching, I saw Pentephraxis at the helm, the sun glinting on his spectacles and the sumpwood burners in his tricorn hat ablaze once more. As if that wasn't enough, the decks of the league ship bristled with the fearsome faces that had stared up at me from the market place. Goblins, cloddertrogs, slavers all, and in their midst, the leering white face of Zelt Pink-Eye, a great curved bow in his hand.

'By the authority invested in me by the United Leagues of Undertown I, Ilmus Pentephraxis, order you to surrender!' the captain's thin, rasping voice rang out. 'Or take the consequences!'

'This is a free ship, leaguesman!' Wind Jackal's voice boomed out in reply. 'We recognize no authority but that of the wind and the storm.'

As if in answer, a volley of arrows and crossbow-bolts whistled through the air towards the *Galerider*. All around me, I could hear the heavy thud and splintering of wood as they embedded themselves in the hull, the mast and the decks.

'More lift, Stone Pilot!' Wind Jackal roared from the helm as his hands danced over the flight-levers.

The *Galerider* soared high as Ramrock doused the flight-rock with the drenching-levers, before wheeling round in a steep arc across the league ship's bow.

'Ready when you are, Master Steg!' the sky pirate captain bellowed.

From the prow of the *Galerider*, Steg Jambles lit the lufwood shaft of the sky ship's great barbed harpoon and sent it hurtling towards the *Scourge of the Weak*! It streaked across the sky, ripping through the spidersilk sails of the league ship, which burst into flames in its fiery wake.

With cries of fury and alarm, the crew cut free the flaming sails and hoisted new ones in their place, while the decks bristled with the crossbows and longbows of slavers jostling for position to fire at the *Galerider* as it sped past. Another volley hissed towards us. At the ironwood gunwales, Garum, the hulking cloddertrog, gave a gurgling scream and clutched his chest as two crossbow bolts found their mark.

'Return fire!' Wind Jackal commanded.

Steg Jambles, Ratbit, Queep and Quint all raised loaded crossbows and let loose a deadly volley in reply. As I watched, ragged gaps suddenly appeared in the ranks of slavers at the balustrade of the league ship. A heavily tattooed flat-head tumbled over, a crossbow bolt buried between his widely spaced eyes, and fell towards the forest below.

The *Galerider*, in full sail, sped off into the endless expanse of treetops. The howling wind in my face made me gasp and grip the railings of the flight-rock platform in terror. I turned my face away and, looking back, saw the league ship turn and give chase. Its fresh sails billowed once more and it rapidly gained on the smaller *Galerider*.

Within moments the *Scourge of the Weak* drew within twenty strides of us, and to my horror I saw Zelt Pink-Eye raise his bow and zero in on Captain Wind Jackal at the helm. Zelt paused, and I held my breath as he trained the bow slowly along the length of the foredeck, as if selecting and rejecting each target in turn, before coming to a halt at

the flight-rock platform.

For an instant I found myself staring into his unblinking pink eye, before he let loose a great barbed arrow.

'*Annghh!*'

Beside me, Ramrock gave a muffled cry and crumpled to the deck, the arrow buried deep in the centre of his back, knocking the flight-rock levers forward as he fell.

Instantly, the rock furnace flared with a brilliant yellow flame and the flight-rock gave a high-pitched whistle as it glowed a deep red. The *Galerider* shuddered and started to go into a downward spiral.

'Ramrock!' Wind Jackal yelled from the helm. 'Do something!'

Almost without thinking, I fell to my knees on

the burning hot flight-rock platform and tore at Ramrock's lifeless body.

'Forgive me,' I murmured as I pulled the heavy gauntlets from his hands and slipped them onto my own. Then, with the heat from the rock furnace burning my face, I wrenched the great hood from his head and slid it down over my shoulders.

The change I felt within me was unforgettable. In that moment, on the burning flight-rock platform of a sinking sky ship, as I looked out of the glass eye-panels of the heavy, protecting hood, I knew that I had found my calling. Here in the midst of the hurricanes and storms of Open Sky, I could stand on this fiery platform and gaze out from the depths of my own personal cavern.

Seizing two cooling rods, I knelt down and thrust them deep into the overheated flight-rock with all the force I could muster. The effect was as exhilarating as it was instantaneous. A great hiss of steam billowed up and streamed past my hooded face, and the rock suddenly cooled and turned buoyant once more.

At the helm, Captain Wind Jackal was quick to react, like the seasoned sky pirate he was. His hands flew over the flight-levers as the *Galerider* shot up into the path of the *Scourge of the Weak*, our razor-like keel slicing the foredeck in two as we passed.

Looking down from the flight-rock deck as the *Galerider* soared away under full sail, my last view of the *Scourge of the Weak* was of the two great lumps of timber – the helm and the prow – separated from one another and tumbling towards the jagged tops of the Deepwoods trees. As it fell it scattered goblins, cloddertrogs, Ilmus Pentephraxis, Zelt Pink-Eye and all to the terrible winds.

Now, seventy-six seasons of the bloodoak later, as I stand here at lonely Riverrise, looking out over the endless Deepwoods, the fierce joy I experienced that day so long ago fills my heart. It was the day that I discovered my calling as a stone pilot and, for a long time, my profession served me well.

I sailed the skies aboard the *Galerider* with Captain Wind Jackal and then, on his passing, with his son, the brave Captain Cloud Wolf – who I'll always remember as Quint, the young sky pirate who rescued me.

After many voyages and some great sorrows, I was proud, in turn, to repay some of the great debt I owed Quint by serving his son, Captain Twig, who

I came to love with all my heart. The voyages we undertook together were some of the most amazing of my long life.

The last time I saw Twig was on this very spot, here at Riverrise many seasons ago, when I used all my knowledge of sky flight to send him hurtling back to the great floating city of Sanctaphrax, to save the Edge from destruction. I know he succeeded, because the spring here at Riverrise flows once more with its life-giving waters, and I wait by the lake it feeds for Twig to return.

I am alone, here with my sadness, the sadness of never having turned termagant, and – more terrible than that – the sadness of losing my dear, dear Twig. It is a sadness that, if I'm not careful, will sink me like a fiery flight-rock sinks a sky ship.

But it must not, because I must wait here at Riverrise. Just in case he returns . . .

THE END